MW01533398

CAMOUFLAGED
HEARTS

N. Viktoria

Copyright © 2024 by **N. Viktoria**

All rights reserved. No part of this publication may be reproduced, distributed or transmitted in any form or by any means, without prior written permission.

N. Viktoria/Alphazuriel Publishing
United States

Publisher's Note: This is a work of fiction. Names, characters, places, and incidents are a product of the author's imagination. . Locales and public names are sometimes used for atmospheric purposes. Any resemblance to actual people, living or dead, or to businesses, companies, events, institutions, or locales is entirely coincidental.

Cover © 2024 Anchorage

Camouflaged Hearts/ N.Viktoria -- 1st ed.
ISBN 9798885090520

CONTENTS

CHAPTER ONE

The bright light from Alecia's laptop rested on her face as she stared at the screen, scrolling through an endless list of matches from her long-forgotten online dating account. The laptop's light illuminated her, casting her in a digital spotlight that seemed a stark contrast to the warmth her cinnamon complexion emanated. She flicked her black, curly locks away from her face, a habitual gesture that punctuated her frustration as she navigated the murky waters of online dating.

Alecia had never imagined that she would find herself doing this again. She could still remember the last guy from one of the numerous dating apps. He was sweet and funny, but honestly, it was his picture that had grabbed her attention. He turned out to be nothing like his display picture, which was a total turn-off. He was still funny, but Alecia had already lost interest. Shaking her head, she brought herself back to reality. Alecia scrolled through an unending list of pitiful matches, rejecting some because she knew there was no way she could be matched with so many men. She soon got bored from her deleting spree, remembering that she had a job that required her to be there before eight in the morning.

Alecia let out a big sigh.

Being an adult was tough, she thought.

She gave the dating app one last look before she planned to close her laptop. Right then, she got a message.

"Hi, how are you?"

She looked at the message, not sure what to say. She checked the photo of the person who sent it and saw a picture of a cat. Weird. This person might think Alecia was

3

looking for something deep. "Sorry, not me," she thought. But she couldn't just ignore the message now that she had seen it.

"Hi. I'm good."

That seemed okay.

She hit send and closed her laptop.

"It's time for Chinese food!" she said out loud.

She opened the food bag, put it on the table, and started to eat with chopsticks. As she ate, she remembered she had a lot to do tomorrow. She didn't hate her job, but she didn't like all the work or her boss much. The good thing was the job paid well. While eating, her phone beeped with a new message. It was her boss, asking her to come in early at 7:30 AM tomorrow for something important.

Alecia slumped into her couch, overwhelmed by the thought of the coming day. "Can tomorrow be any more stressful?" she muttered to herself. Suddenly, her appetite vanished, and she found herself having to store the leftovers in the fridge, despite having looked forward to finishing

5

her meal. As she placed her unfinished Chinese food inside, she was greeted by an assortment of other uneaten meals, from spaghetti to takeout from various restaurants. It dawned on her that it had been ages since she had cooked a proper meal. Caught up in her work, she barely found time for herself.

After closing the fridge, Alecia dragged her feet to her room, preparing for bed. Following a quick shower, she slipped into her PJs and climbed into bed, half-jokingly hoping not to die in her sleep since she felt she hadn't lived her life to the fullest yet. Just as she was about to drift off, she snapped her eyes open, realizing she hadn't called Noah, her boyfriend. Despite her hectic schedule, Alecia and Noah managed to keep their relationship going, even living together at one point. However, Noah's recent promotion meant he had to move, and Alecia couldn't follow due to her job commitments. Lately, she had been contemplating moving to be with him, missing him terribly and aware that their relationship had been facing some challenges.

Alecia dialed Noah's number, waiting impatiently for him to pick up. The call ended without an answer, and she tried again, a second, third, and fourth time, each call ending without any response. It was unusual because he typically answered, but she assumed he must be asleep, too exhausted to notice his phone ringing. With a sigh, trying not to overthink, she sent him a text to let him know she had called. She set her alarm for 6:30 AM, placed her phone on the nightstand, and drifted off to sleep.

The next morning, Alecia arrived at the office just in time, the first one there, to her surprise. The office was eerily quiet, contrasting sharply with its usual busy atmosphere, always filled with clients seeking help. As a legal secretary, her work was endless, from drafting legal documents and attending court to filing and giving legal advice, often with little recognition. She started to think she might need a break but wondered how to even bring up the subject with her boss, who had yet to arrive, despite it being past 7:30 AM.

As the cleaner and some of her coworkers began to settle in, Alecia thought about her challenging relationships with some of the lawyers. Many of them were arrogant, a trait she found off-putting, so she tended to avoid them.

"Hey, Alicia," Mr. Montez, one of the cleaners, called to her.

"Hi, Mr. Montez."

"You're in early today."

"Well, yeah. The boss asked me to."

"Oh, he did? What for?"

"Not sure. But I'm sure it's important."

"Okay then, I'll catch you later."

With Montez gone, everything got boring again. Alecia had no choice but to take out her phone. She checked for a text from Noah but there was no reply. She wanted to call him but decided to wait. She thought maybe he was still asleep and would text her back later.

Alecia put her phone on the desk and started tapping it, trying to keep herself from getting bored. She had deleted all her social media apps so she wouldn't get distracted at work, which now made her phone seem pretty useless. She remembered the guy from last night and wondered if he had replied. She thought about reinstalling the app but wasn't sure.

Just then, her boss walked in. Alecia quickly hid her phone and went to greet him.

"Mr. Reynolds. Good morning," she said, hoping he might apologize for making her come in early for no reason. But he just handed her his suitcase instead.

"Hold this for me, will you?" Reynolds held the suitcase to her face.

"Sure," Alecia took it from him, trotting behind him as they entered Reynolds's office.

"Sir, I came to the office by 7:30 AM like you asked me to but I didn't see you."

"And why would you expect me to be here so early?"

Alecia was stunned by his reply.

What did he just say? He's got to be joking with that reply.

"You sent me a text last night, sir…" She took out her phone from her pocket, tapped the messages icon and showed him his text. "…right there, sir. That's the text you sent."

"Oh, this text. I accidentally sent it to you but deleted it the second I did. I guess the 5G network is worth the hype. The text was originally meant for Montez, whom I resent the text to."

Alecia's feet suddenly felt ice cold. She had a strong urge to scream, wishing the ground would swallow her up. While lost in her thoughts, she could hear Mr. Reynolds speaking but couldn't really understand him. He started staring at her, likely wondering what was going on with her.

"Could you please repeat what you said, sir?"

"Don't tell me you didn't hear a single thing I said," he sighed, and pinched the bridge of his nose. "I said I need you to help me type some documents for a..., print out four copies and send them to my office. I need them in less than an hour from now."

"Less than an hour?"

"Yes. What you'll be typing won't be much. I'll send the details to your desk right away."

"Alright," Alecia dropped his suitcase on his desk and left.

Alecia checked her email, finding a three-page document from her boss, contradicting his assurance that there

16

wouldn't be much for her to type. She took a deep breath and buried her face in her hands, reminding herself, "This is what you signed up for, Alecia. You just have to go through with it." She prepared herself to tackle the task ahead.

As Alecia's favorite time of the day arrived, she felt a wave of happiness at the thought of going home, even though she would be back the next day. On the other hand, Noah still hadn't replied to her text, which had never happened before. Usually, he would at least send an apology if he was too busy. Despite wanting to call him, she hesitated, fearing her own reaction. She wondered if something was wrong, why he hadn't called back or replied. Slumping on the couch, phone in hand, she noticed the text from her boss the night before, which only added to her annoyance. Reflecting on the embarrassment of the morning, she deleted the message.

Alecia turned to her trusty laptop which was sitting pretty on the kitchen counter. She remembered the mysterious guy from last night and their half-baked conversation. She headed to the counter, opened her laptop, and logged into the app. She noticed five extra matches from just last night which made her giggle. Alecia checked to see if the stranger had replied, which he had. She then clicked open inbox to read his text.

"That's great.

What's your name? I'm Ash.

You're pretty by the way."

Alecia's cheeks warmed up unexpectedly at the compliment, despite hearing it many times before. While she didn't usually feel flattered by such comments anymore and remained committed to Noah, his recent behavior left her craving a distraction. She contemplated Ash's message. It wouldn't be cheating if she gave in fully to have a conversation with him, but on the other hand, a conversation with Ash might be the distraction she needed to get her mind off the situation going on with Noah.

Ash. What a weird name.

No. That sounded too rude.

She deleted the text and thought of another reply.

"Hey, Ash.

I'm Alecia.

Thank you for the compliment."

That was better.

Ash wasn't online, leaving Alecia torn between going to his profile to stalk him a bit more or getting on with her routine.

21

Just as she was about to get up, his status changed from offline to typing.

Oh no. Oh no! What is he typing?! Alecia panicked.

"Alecia, huh?
What a pretty name."

Now my name is pretty too?

"Yeah, it is. Don't you think so too?"

"I mean it's just a name."

"Oh, okay, my bad.

I'd like to get to know more about you."

"What do you want to know?" Alecia asked

"Everything.

Well, not everything.

Just the basics.

Where you're from, what you do for a

living.

Stuff like that."

"Okay.

Well, I'm a legal secretary.

I work at a law firm in NYC."

"Wow. NYC?

That's where I stay.

Well, I don't exactly live here.

I move around a lot.

So where are you from?"

"Well, I'm both African and American.

I was born in the US but my dad is

from Africa.

Nigeria to be precise."

"Nigeria?

Wow!"

"What?" she asked

"Nothing.

It's just… I got back from my

deployment to Nigeria a few weeks back."

"Really?

That's cool.

And why were you sent there?"

"We were asked to help fight against

these terrorist groups. I don't know if

you've heard of Boko Haram." Ash replied

"Oh, yeah, I've heard of them.

I honestly don't know what people gain

when they cause so much harm to people.

I'm surprised you're a soldier.

What's a soldier doing on a dating app?"

"Trying to find love, I guess.

I am not usually able to go

out and meet people often,

so I figured I'd try meeting people online."

"Well, for someone who has tried online

dating, trust me when I say you're

gonna need all the luck you'll get."

"Why do you say so?"

"Because most people here are catfishes.

Fakes pretending to be something they're

not."

"Are you a catfish?"

"Hell, no!"

"Then I guess I'm safe."

Alecia suddenly realized she had been texting Ash for almost an hour without noticing.

Normally, she didn't engage much in texting, but texting Ash felt different; it was easy and comfortable. Even though she felt guilty for enjoying a conversation with someone other than Noah, whom she still loved, there was something intriguing about Ash that she couldn't quite identify.

This new feeling was something Alecia

found herself wanting to explore more,

despite the loyalty she felt towards Noah.

CHAPTER TWO

Alecia never understood the idea of
expressing love on just one day instead of
every day. However, she embraced
Valentine's Day traditions because Noah,
her partner, enjoyed them. They've
celebrated with dinner dates and themed
parties, though Alecia would prefer a quiet
night at home watching romance movies
together. She believed in sacrificing her
own preferences for the happiness of
others, a testament to her belief that life
involves mutual sacrifices. This year, Noah
had promised to visit her apartment on

Valentine's Day to do whatever Alecia wished, a change from their usual routine of following Noah's preferences. Excited yet indecisive about the day's activities, she searched online for simple and romantic Valentine's ideas but found nothing appealing. At that moment, a text from Ash appears on her screen.

"Hey.

How're you?

It's been a while.

Are you back from work?"

"Not now, Ash. I'm busy."

Alecia decides to ignore Ash's text, letting the notification linger on her screen until it vanishes. She continues her search for the perfect way to spend a 'minimalist Valentine's Day' with your partner, browsing through various blog posts for ideas. However, her frustration mounts as none of the suggestions match what she's looking for. Just then, Noah calls, and Alecia quickly answers, eager to hear his voice and perhaps find a break from her growing frustration.

"Hey, babe. I was just looking up a few ideas for our Valentine's date. So far, none of the ideas I've come across matches my taste."

"Yeah… about that date. I don't think I can make it in time for Valentine's Day."

Alecia's heart skips a beat. "What… What do you mean you won't be able to make it? We've been planning this for a long time and now you're bailing on me," she struggles to hold back her tears.

"I'm sorry, babe. It's not me, it's work. I just have a lot to do. I've got a meeting with my director concerning some complaints from the lower staff and I don't think we'll be done in time for me to get to New York City."

"Oh, I guess in that case, I'll just have to spend Valentine's Day alone."

"I'm so sorry, babe. I promise to make it up to you when we can finally see each other."

"And when will that be?" Alecia asks, heartbroken.

Noah doesn't say anything. Alecia can hear distant muttering from the background and a lady giggling. She becomes alarmed.

"Noah! Noah!" Alecia calls his name, almost yelling. Deep down, she was frightened.

Maybe the female voice I just heard is a co-worker, Alecia tries to convince herself even though she knows Noah gets home from work an hour before she does. So, whoever that was… wherever that voice came from, had to be from his apartment.

"Hey, Babe. I'm sorry. Microwave emergency," he chuckles stylishly.

"Who was that, Noah?"

"Who was what?"

"That girl I heard. Who was she?"

"What are you talking about, Alecia?"

And there it was, Alecia's gut feeling confirmed. She had a knack for detecting when Noah wasn't being truthful, whether by his facial expressions or, in cases like this, the tone of his voice. Despite his efforts to hide it, Alecia could sense the dishonesty in his voice, a clear indication he was lying and trying hard to conceal it.

"You know I can tell when you lie. And right now, honestly, Noah, you're doing a terrible job."

"Um… I'll call you back later. My boss is calling."

"Noah, don't you…"

Noah ends the call before she can finish, leaving her confused with no words to describe how she feels. How long has he been with her? Who was she? Was she black like me? What did she have that I didn't? What did Noah see in her?

Just as she's about to wallow in her misery,
Ash comes to the rescue.

"Hey, are you okay?"

She looks at her screen and a smile crack on
her lips.

*Oh, Ash, I don't deserve you. I deserve to be left
alone in this cruel dark world. She thought.*

Alecia doesn't have the urge to reply, so she
gets up and goes to the bedroom. She hears
the notification bell ring again. There's no
doubt it's Ash's text.

"Come on! Don't you know when someone is trying to ignore you?" She muses

"I was wondering if you're free on Valentine's Day.
So we could meet up." Ash texts

Alecia finds herself at a crossroads, gazing at her laptop screen, uncertain of how to respond to Ash. Initially, she had plans for Valentine's Day, but those were unexpectedly canceled. Now, she contemplates whether to lie to Ash or to seize this opportunity to prioritize her own happiness by giving Ash a chance. Her fingers hover above the keyboard, reflecting her indecision.

Come on, Alecia. Sometimes, you have to think about yourself and no one else. Noah is a jerk, and you don't deserve him.

"No, I don't have any plans for Valentine."

"Great!
So can we meet then?"

"Yeah, meeting up sounds great.
What restaurant do you have in mind?"

"Um, I don't know how this might

sound to you, but I'm not the kind of guy

that fancies restaurant.

Lol."

"No. No. I get it.

I'm also not the kind of girl that

fancy restaurants.

I'm more of a private date kinda girl."

"Okay, then.

So, how about we meet up, and I

show you what I have planned."

"Is it gonna be a surprise?" Alecia asks

"Don't you like surprises?!"

"No, it's not that.

I'm just not used to being intentionally

surprised.

But I'm open to whatever you have

planned."

"Oh, thank God.

I'll pick you up at eight then.

It's a date."

Alecia is taken aback by Ash's last text and

unsure how to respond. She notices he has

gone offline, which puzzles her. Why did

he leave so suddenly? After a moment, she

gathers her courage and types 'it's a date!',

41

sending the message without looking too closely at her screen. Suddenly, Ash is online again and typing. Alecia feels anxious, wondering what he will say next. Then, a smiley face emoji pops up from his side of the chat. She is confused at first. Why just a smiley after all that waiting? Then it hits her; maybe Ash is just as nervous as she is about texting. It is kind of comforting to think he might be feeling the same way. However, it is hard to be sure about someone's true feelings through texting. She just has to meet him to find out.

Alecia feels out of place as she looks at herself in the mirror, dressed up for what was supposed to be a casual outing. Despite the effort to keep things simple, her outfit, makeup, and jewelry made her feel like she was going to a very formal event. She recalled how Noah always wanted her to look her best, desiring the attention and admiration of others whenever they were together. 'I want people to turn their heads whenever we walk past them.

"I want them to know I have a girl and my girl is hot," Noah would always say.

Maybe that's why he was cheating on her.

Maybe people didn't stare so much

anymore and wonder; wow! I can't believe they're a couple. Oh my God, I want to be just like her and be his girl. Or maybe she just didn't do it for him anymore. Just like stale bread.

Come on, Alecia, you shouldn't be talking to yourself like this. You're a queen! And if Noah doesn't see that, then he's straight-up stupid, Alecia tries to console herself.

Sitting on her bed, Alecia catches her reflection in the mirror, resisting the urge to check the time on her phone beside her, fearing it was already past eight.

Punctuality had become important to her, a habit formed under Noah's influence, who used to set their meeting times an hour early. Now, as she contemplates the timing of her date with Ash, she wonders if she should have planned for a later hour. Her phone vibrates, snapping her out of her thoughts. It's Ash, and he's already outside her apartment, ready for their date.

She rushes to the window, hoping to find him, but for someone she hasn't seen in real life, she finds it hard to spot him among the other people.

"Calm down, Alecia, there's nothing to be nervous about," she assures herself while taking deep breaths.

Alecia steps back from the window, bracing herself to meet Ash. She's aware of the uncertainties that come with online dating. There's a chance Ash won't live up to the expectations she's set in her mind, or he might be completely different from his online persona, similar to a past online date experience. Furthermore, she can't shake off the worry that Ash might not be who he claims to be at all, fearing the worst-case scenario where her search for companionship leads her into danger.

What if he's a serial killer who, all thanks to my desperate need for attention, has found his next victim?

46

"Whoa! Okay now, Alecia. You're starting to get a little overboard there with all that thinking. It's Valentine's Day, Ash is a good guy, go have some fun."

Alecia collects her purse, keys, and phone, confidently stepping into the hallway. She double-checks that her door is properly locked before heading to the elevator, where she encounters an old lady. The old lady smiles at her and seems to take note of Alecia's outfit. Alecia wonders what could be going on in the old lady's mind — maybe criticizing her outfit or her makeup. But Alecia isn't shaken by any possible

47

opinions. Nothing can ruin the surge of confidence she felt at that moment.

"Going out for Valentine's I see," the old lady says with a wide grin.

"Yeah, and I'm super nervous," Alecia tries not to lay all her problems out on this stranger.

"Well, you shouldn't be. You are gorgeous, honey; I'm sure whoever you're going out with will love you."

Love? Isn't that a bit too sudden? She thought.

Alecia smiles, thankful for her kind words. "Thank you."

Alecia steps out into the lobby, scanning the area for Ash, wondering how she'll recognize someone she's never seen in person. Just as she's about to text him, she spots someone approaching her.

"Hi, there. You're Alecia, right?"

"Yeah, that's me."

"I'm Ash."

"Ash?"

49

Holy shit! Ash is white.

CHAPTER THREE

Alecia's eyes scanned Ash's features, from his ruffled brown hair to his jade green eyes to his entire outfit. He was wearing a gray coat with a black scarf around his neck, owing to the fact that it had been freezing lately. A brow lifted on his face, and he narrowed his eyes at her as she stared. Meanwhile, she continued to gape at him like she'd just seen a ghost—a very tall and incredibly good-looking ghost.

"Alecia?" he called out, tilting his head.

She quickly snapped out of her trance. She sure as hell hadn't been expecting a white guy. Well, he'd said all those things about Africa and all. She wouldn't have thought a white person would know so much about Nigeria and other African countries.

"Oh, I'm sorry, I was just…"

"Surprised?"

She nodded, not wanting to tell him her exact reasons for being so dumbfounded. "Yup, exactly."

The corners of his lips curved into a lopsided grin as he took in her appearance. "You look really good in person," he said.

A blush threatened to creep up Alecia's cheeks, but she waved it off as fast as she could. "Oh please, you're just so into flattery."

He smiled charmingly. "Well, I hope it's working."

She pouted playfully. "You're getting there."

He chuckled, allowing her the pleasure of noticing his pearly white teeth and how the corners of his eyes crinkled. He was, dare she say it, absolutely breathtaking. It made her wonder if she should give him a compliment as well. He had taken out some time to make her feel good about herself tonight, and he deserved one too. But she didn't know why she felt she'd be exposing her thoughts too much if she did so. Maybe she could try a curt, less constructive compliment? One that didn't have to do with his perfect smile, his sleek fashion sense, or those eyes that were suddenly seeming more green now than they had looked earlier.

He opened the door of his car for her like any gentleman would, and she stepped in before he joined her in the driver's seat. Alecia couldn't deny the trepidation at the bottom of her gut as she played with her fingers nervously while he revved the engine and started the car. Her brain was literally burning out from contemplating which compliment to give him.

Maybe he didn't even want compliments.

Don't be silly, Alecia. Everyone wants compliments, she reprimanded herself.

"Um… you look great too…" she finally stuttered under her breath. She then caught a glimpse of him from the corner of her eye; however, his face was still focused on the road. Was he going to say anything?

"Thanks. Was beginning to think you didn't like my outfit," he said, causing her to panic.

"No, why would you think that?"

"Well, for starters, the way you were staring at me." He finally shifted his gaze to her.

She looked away quickly. "I was just surprised. Like you didn't show me your pic on your profile."

Without waiting for his reply, she changed the subject, turning to face him. "So, where are we going?"

She was curious and excited but still a bit cautious. Ash was still a stranger, and it wasn't prudent to just hop into a stranger's car and let them take you wherever they wanted without knowing the details. Ash could have been a kidnapper for all she knew.

"I said it was a surprise," he teased. "But I can assure you I'm not planning on doing anything illegal." He shot her a look.

How had he read her mind?

"I wasn't thinking that," she said and reclined back into the seat. She heard him laugh from her side, and unconsciously, a smile began to etch on her lips. She had to admit, she loved how confident he was.

New York City was usually bright this late at night, and the celebration of love in the air was only adding to the exuberant aura. Driving past the lights, Ash felt relaxed; his life had been one big adventure for the past two years, and now that he was taking a break, he was glad to have someone to spend the days with—even though sometimes, the way she stared at him was a bit weird. He wondered if she was expecting something better or worse from their first encounter. Alecia, on the other hand, was lost out of the window the entire ride. She let the chilly breeze find its way to her skin while she cuddled deeper into her coat.

The buildings were decorated with twinkling lights, and the streets were bubbling with couples. Couples. Her smile dropped at the thought of Noah and what he was up to tonight. The female voice she'd heard from the phone echoed in her head, but she didn't let her mind drift any further. She knew if she thought about Noah's betrayal, she'd be hurt, and it would be difficult for her to heal. Tonight would be ruined.

Tonight was supposed to be her reward for working her butt off at work all month. She was meant to relax and let all the negative thoughts out, like Noah—and that stupid presentation she had tomorrow, which she was scantily prepared for. She took a deep breath. She'd see where the night would take her.

The amusement park.

The night had taken her to the amusement park! Ash halted the vehicle at the parking lot, but Alecia was way too busy staring at the vast, radiant park, wide-eyed. She couldn't remember the last time she'd actually come just to have fun at an amusement park. In fact, she couldn't recall the last time she'd felt her stomach tingle with the anticipation of trying out new rides in the place.

"Oh my God! An amusement park?!" she exclaimed, looking around at the colorful

61

rides and letting the mixed smell of different snacks penetrate her nose. Mmm, popcorn...

"Wow, you're really excited?" he asked.

She looked back at him. "You really don't want to know the last time I came here."

He chuckled, and soon, they both alighted from his car and began to walk to the park. As she went by, she sighted a bunch of cheesy, irritating couples, but she ignored them. Goodness knew what Noah was up to tonight. She picked out her phone and stared at his number. The only way to find out was to give him a call.

She instantly snapped back to reality. What was she doing? She placed the phone back in her purse. He didn't deserve to be running through her thoughts. He didn't. Forget about Noah for one night, will you Alecia?

"So, are you going to tell me what plans were canceled tonight?" Ash asked, turning around and handing her a piece of cotton candy. She accepted it with a big smile.

"It's nothing important, trust me." She shrugged, tearing out some cotton and eating it.

"Oh really?" They proceeded away from the stand, and she'd noticed he hadn't gotten anything for himself.

She quirked a brow at him. "Don't you like candy?"

He nodded. "Oh, I do very much."

"So it's the cotton ones you don't like then?"

Ash shrugged. "Eh, I'm not in the mood for sweet stuff tonight."

Ash wasn't a big fan of sugary food. He was overly cautious of his health, and so he believed that the Halloween candies and cake icings he'd eaten as a kid were enough.

Alecia rolled her eyes, and he found himself liking it when she acted more carefree around him. "It's Valentine's Day! Literally the day of 'sweet stuff', Ash."

He laughed before looking back in front. "Why were you on a dating site anyways?"

She looked up. "Me? Well…"

The truth was that Alecia didn't have an answer to that. Besides, the real question should be, why was she on a dating site when she already had a boyfriend? Well, ever since Noah had left town, it had gotten very lonely in Alecia's apartment. And she didn't have many friends. Okay, she didn't have any friends, plus she was way too busy to go out and socialize. And so what did the legal secretary think would be the solution?

Find-your-dream-match dot com!

And soon, many other apps and sites with unbelievably corny names.

"It's nothing," she began explaining. "I guess, it just got lonely in my apartment after Noah left…"

Ash looked at her interestedly, and she internally scolded herself. What was that about not oversharing with people she had just met?

"I'm sorry, I talk too much sometimes."

"Please go on, you got me interested now."

She hesitated. "I'm actually not that comfortable with being open right now."

She hoped her honesty hadn't been rude.

He took the cotton candy from her hand and smiled at her. "How about this? I dare you to go on one of the rides. If you do so without backing out, you don't have to tell me, but if you're too scared, then you'll have to tell me everything about this Noah person."

Alecia scoffed. "That's it? These rides aren't even that scary." She spotted a carousel and scoffed again. Please.

He smirked, placing both his hands in his coat pockets. "Oh, so it's a deal?"

He seemed oddly confident, but she was sure it wouldn't be a problem. From her last memory of the amusement park, the rides weren't so terrifying. She didn't know what all the fuss was about. Was it the rollercoasters he was referring to?

"Last time I checked, Ash, I have no problem with heights, so yeah, it's a deal," she said.

She had left Ash with the responsibility of picking their ride, and oh, he took his sweet time scrutinizing all of them. But that was until she saw something. It was a massive ride, and she might just be hallucinating, but had those people being tossed around on it? Her heart skipped a beat when Ash's eyes moved to the ride, and a daunting smirk formed on his lips.

No no no no, Ash. Don't say it, she thought.

He looked at her, and he had that smile on where the corners of his eyes crinkled.

However, this time, it was fraught with mischief.

"I like that ride, it's cool, don't you think?"

She stammered. "Ash, it's-what's um, I think it's a bit too expensive. I'm on a tight budget, let's choose a different one."

"Chickening out already?" He pulled out his wallet. "You don't have to worry. It's on me."

Alecia's heart was pounding furiously in her chest, and she gulped down—hard. This guy was even more sly than she thought. But the smug grin on his face forced her to swallow all her fear and walk forward. "Alright then."

She turned around with feigned flair. "The ride isn't gonna ride itself."

He stood there, watching her with what appeared to be confusion tinged with amusement. Ash knew she was terrified of the ride, but why was she suddenly agreeing? He didn't want her to take on something she couldn't handle because of him. He watched her turn and catch a glimpse of it once again, and her face was replete with anxiety. He was sure she was going to back out.

"Okay. If you say so."

He finally joined her, and before they knew it, they were done buying the tickets and were now standing next in line to get on the ride. Her hands were frozen, and no, it wasn't because of the weather. She rubbed them together surreptitiously and sneaked a peek at Ash. He was staring up ahead, not in the least bit daunted by what was before them. Well, what else could she expect from an army officer? He had probably seen much worse than a... a human yoyo?

73

Apparently, they were meant to sit in pairs on the bottom while the machine carried them and tossed them around like a yoyo. But they didn't have to worry; it was "safe" and "hadn't had any records of death since twenty-sixteen"—according to the announcer. Her body stiffened, and at his words, the gesture only caused Ash to laugh from her side.

She watched the ride and heard the sound of people screaming, and suddenly, she became weak. Yeah, they had probably been screaming with excitement, but they were screaming nonetheless. She couldn't do this.

74

"Sure you wanna do this, sweetheart?" Ash asked sarcastically, leaning towards her ear, still, she could sense the worried undertone in his voice. Her brain was so befuddled by the fear of the ride that she could hardly comprehend the term of endearment Ash had used to refer to her just now.

She turned around, completely ignoring the line waiting behind them. She whispered to Ash, "I can't do this. What kind of a ride is that?" She turned back and grimaced at the towering deathtrap.

"You don't have to ride if you don't want to," he said, and she nodded. Yeah, it wouldn't kill her to lose the dare, but it just might do so if she didn't. Besides, what was the harm in sharing just a part of her life with Ash? He seemed eager to know it anyways—which was flattering since people weren't usually this interested in knowing much about her life.

Irritated complaints began to rise from the people waiting in line behind them. Some said that if Alecia was too scared to ride, she should just leave, and others—which she was guessing were singles—told them that "the lovebirds couldn't just do as they pleased just 'cause it was Valentine's Day."

Lovebirds? Had Ash and her really looked like they were in love? Suddenly, she became self-conscious as her mind put two and two together. Of course, people would think they were together. It was obvious with all the whispering, and they couldn't forget that the both of them were here, in an amusement park, at night, on Valentine's Day. It was all just a simple misunderstanding. She was about to explain to the person that the two of them weren't really together, but then Ash stopped her, quickly grabbing her hand and leading her out of the line. As soon as they got to a safe spot, away from the angry mob, they stared at each other and immediately burst into a fit of laughter. Money was wasted, and she completely made a fool of herself there, but the experience was worth it. In all, she was just glad she didn't kill herself on that ride.

"So," Ash said after they had finished laughing, shoveling his hands into his coat pockets. Are you ready to start talking?"

CHAPTER FOUR

Over ice cream, Alecia sat at one of the benches and talked about Noah to Ash. She told him how they first met outside a court where she'd gone with her boss, and how they started meeting up from there. Then, she pushed further to add how they started to fall for each other before he'd soon decided to move in and live with her. Ash listened quietly as she told him about Noah's distant behavior lately, ever since he left the city, and she braced herself and spilled the fact that she suspected he was cheating on her.

"Don't be mad but that's part of the reason I agreed to go on this date with you. I was hurt by Noah and was looking for a way to, you know, get my mind off things," she explained.

Ash took a scoop of the ice cream Alecia had persuaded him to get. Surprisingly, she was very good at convincing people. "It's alright. It sounds like you really love this Noah guy."

She shrugged. She didn't feel comfortable talking about her feelings like this. "Well, I do." She rubbed her fingers together. "But I feel like I shouldn't anymore."

She let out a deep sigh. "It's just. I don't know. It just feels as if everything's messed up in my life right now. I don't want to think how much mental pressure it'll be after dealing with Noah's betrayal, then I'll have to go to that stupid job where my boss doesn't even consider me... and then there's this presentation I have tomorrow that I haven't been prepared for."

"Tomorrow?" her confidante asked, and she realized she'd been yapping away. Though, at least he was listening.

"Yeah," she said. "But don't worry. I'll figure it out. But tonight, I just want to have a break from work."

He smirked. "Yeah, I totally get that."

She looked at him. "I've been going on and on about myself. Tell me about you."

He relaxed an arm on the back of the chair. "Not much. I'm free in the meantime, and that's why I'm actually here. Last Valentine's Day, I was still in Africa, getting bitten by a snake." He narrowed his eyes as if recalling the event.

She laughed. "Oh my God. Are you okay?"

"Nah, I'm afraid the snake bite was pretty poisonous." He shook his head. "I didn't make it out alive," he said with a somber tone.

She hit him on the arm as soon as she noticed his sarcasm. "Rude! I meant were you okay? That time!"

They both laughed, and she inwardly hoped that this carefree moment would last forever. She loved the way Ash always lightened up the mood. He'd made her feel completely relaxed after a while, and she couldn't thank him enough for that. The air hit her skin like ice, and she shivered slightly. The freezing breeze increased, and now, her teeth were chattering. She rubbed her hands together to create friction, but goodness, the numbness couldn't seem to go away. She would kill for some hot cocoa right now.

"I knew when you asked for ice cream, you'd had the intention of killing us," Ash joked, and she giggled.

"I know it's my fault, but I have hot cocoa back at home if you're interested."

84

He shook his head matter-of-factly. "Um, I would definitely love some."

She laughed, and they both stood up. Ash led her to his car, and they were deep in a conversation filled with laughs and jokes until they stopped right in front of Alecia's apartment.

"I hope you got marshmallows with the hot cocoa?" he asked, leaning on the wall as she unlocked her door.

She tilted her head to him. "What if I don't?"

"Then we'll have to work something out. What's hot cocoa without marshmallows?"

She laughed. Alecia also thought hot chocolate shouldn't be served without marshmallows. It was her favorite topping. "Don't worry, I'm not an animal. I've got some in the fridge."

Pushing the door open, she walked inside, and Ash followed, taking in the apartment. It wasn't pretty, but it was well kept—had been ever since Noah moved in with her. Before that, Alecia would have never given a shit about if her bed wasn't made or if there was a pizza box on the floor. She hadn't wanted him to think she was disorganized, and so she'd turned the whole place around. Now, it was a small one-bedroom studio apartment with a queen-sized bed and a working desk. Then, there was the closet, a kitchen, which was just enough to store her skinflint budget food stuff, and the bathroom. So, if you ask her, that was part of the little good things she'd gotten from dating Noah. She opened her cabinet and, luckily, amidst all the sad excuses for groceries, the cocoa powder was still intact. It was the only thing bought in bulk, so it had lasted for more than two months now. She soon began to make the hot beverage, and after a few minutes, she was back in the room with steaming hot cocoa in two cups. When she got there, she heard a message come into her laptop, but Ash had already found it.

"A text just came in. It's from your boss," he informed her. "He hopes you're ready for the huge presentation tomorrow."

She became a bit worried. It was already late, probably twelve A.M., and she still hadn't gotten ready for it. Her stomach churned at the thought of what Mr. Reynolds would do to her if she messed up tomorrow.

"Yeah, it's already late, and I'm tired. Maybe I'll find out how I'll talk to him tomorrow." She was being irresponsible; she knew that. But Mr. Reynolds needed to know that all humans need breaks, even the ones that work for him.

"Do you want to risk losing your job?" Ash took a cup from the tray and sipped.

She plopped on the bed, exhausted. "What do you suggest I do?"

He placed the cup on the desk. "Why don't I help you prepare for your presentation?

That way, you don't have to do it all by yourself."

She was taken aback by his suggestion. "You want to help me out?"

He shrugged. "Sure, unless you have a problem with it?"

"No, not at all, it's just that it's late, and I still have to get up by six and get to work early tomorrow…"

"Come on, it won't take much time." The way he looked at her with those jade green eyes was enough to soften her. And something about the way some strands of his hair fell on his face was urging her to run her fingers through them. But of course, she couldn't do that. It might just push him away.

And deep down, she knew she wanted him to stay.

"Okay fine, I'll prepare for it with you," she said with a defeated voice. "So where do we start?"

Ash and Alecia had practiced for the presentation meeting the entire night. It hadn't taken long for Alecia's eyelids to start becoming heavy, but Ash had decided to go sit next to her on the floor, next to her bed, so she would concentrate on the questions he'd asked her and wouldn't drift off to sleep. However, that idea had totally backfired.

It turned out Ash's warm body in very close proximity to her was able to send her into a comfortable, cozy sleep faster than Spanish Soap Operas could.

Unfortunately, her beautiful sleep was interrupted by the bright light from her window forcing its way into her eyes. Alecia blocked the rays away with her hand and turned to snuggle into her pillow—her very hard pillow that smelled so good. Since when did she start dipping her pillows in heavenly smelling cologne? Slowly, her eyelids fluttered open, and she realized that she wasn't on her bed. She was shamelessly snuggling Ash's arm, and that too while laying her head on his shoulder. Her eyes wandered over his stunning features. His jawline, his lips, his hair... she observed how ruffled his hair was. It wouldn't hurt anyone if she just ran her fingers through it, now would it? Besides, he wouldn't know. He was asleep.

Her hands approached his hair slowly and were about to touch it when he woke up abruptly. She retreated immediately and pulled away from him.

"When did we fall asleep?" he asked, rubbing his eyes.

She comprehended what he was saying, and that was when it hit her. Her presentation!

"What's the time?" she demanded, getting up quickly and dashing to get her phone. 7:45!

Oh shit! She was supposed to be at work by seven! It was over. Mr. Reynolds would definitely kill her!

"Oh crap, I forgot about your presentation!" Ash said, running his hand through his hair. He then suggested that she got herself ready while he helped her with the other stuff, but she refused.

"You don't have to worry about it," she said, but he insisted. Ultimately, she agreed, and soon enough, she was ready to leave. He'd also insisted that he take her to work in his car, and she also agreed. In not less than thirty minutes, they arrived at the law firm. With the way Ash was driving, she was scared they would have gotten a speeding ticket. But the cops couldn't give a ticket to a soldier... right? When they stopped, Alecia judged from the number of people who were already present at the firm that she was extremely late.

Ash wished her good luck, and she smiled back at him before alighting and scurrying to the building.

When she got to the meeting room, she slowly opened the door and immediately,

all eyes turned to her. The place was full,
and it turned out they'd already started
without her. She looked up to see someone
already giving a presentation. She wasn't
sure if she should have gone before him or
if she'd made it right in time and was
actually after him, but she was certain she
was in big trouble. Cautiously, she took a
seat next to Mr. Reynolds, and as she did so,
he shot her a sour look—one that sent a
shiver down her spine. Oh, I'm definitely in
big trouble, she said to herself.

Much to her luck, she was called to give her
presentation. She was glad all her practice
wasn't in vain. As she spoke in front of

97

everyone, the intimidating look Mr. Reynolds continued to give her made her stumble on some of her words, but she picked herself up from where she stopped and continued. She should be glad he was even letting her speak.

After the meeting, she exited the room, and she was in the hallway when her boss called her:

"Alecia."

She halted in her steps. "Yes, sir."

"What was all that about?"

"What do you mean, sir?"

"You know what I mean, Alecia. You're an hour late? You should thank your stars. Your presentation was good; if not, you would have been packing up your stuff by now." He snapped his fingers.

She looked down. "I'm sorry, sir. I won't make that mistake again."

"Yes, you better not because now, you're on probation. Next time you do something like this again, you'll be asked to leave," he dropped the bomb and left her to ponder on what he just said. She frowned. He was acting like she did this every day. The last time she came super early, he hadn't even appreciated that. Her hands balled into a fist. Goodness knew she was fed up with that man. Now, she was on probation? Her job was at stake, and all this wouldn't have happened if she hadn't stayed up late with Ash.

Though it was his preparation that had saved her. Without him, she would have been packing up by now, as Mr. Reynolds had said.

She sighed. She didn't know how to feel at the moment. It was probably just all her fault. She was the one who was way too desperate to go out for Valentine's Day last night.

But now, she decided, she'd take her job much more seriously. She wouldn't let anything worsen her situation.

Immediately, she got a text from Ash:

"Hey.

How did the meeting go?"

She sighed and typed a reply, not wanting to give out all the details, or tell him about her probation.

"Luckily, I got away with it.
He said he liked my presentation."

He replied quickly:

"Oh thank goodness.
I was worried you got into trouble.
Because of me."

She stared at the text. Hanging out with Ash had almost made her lose her job, but it wasn't his fault. He was only trying to help. And besides, it had been long since she had her blood pumping like this. So maybe it had been worth it. She sent a reply:

"It's not your fault.

I'm the one who wasn't prepared.

You were just trying to help.

Thanks."

A new message beeped in, but she kept her phone away and headed off to work. Probation, she scoffed inwardly.

CHAPTER FIVE

It turned out that Mr. Reynolds had been serious about the probation thing, and so Alecia decided to pay more attention to her job and avoid anything that would possibly jeopardize it. Fortunately for her, Ash had said he had some work to take care of in New Jersey, and so he'd been out for three days. It was a good thing because she knew that with Ash and his witty, fun nature around, she wouldn't be able to get anything done. Though she still sort of missed him—even after their long chats and calls. It was embarrassing, she couldn't stay a moment without talking to him, even though they'd only known each other for a week.

"Yes, Sir," she said to her boss who was on the other line. "Seven P.M. prompt. Got it." When she was done with the call, she shoved the phone into her pocket and walked in with her Chinese takeout secured in her hands. Then, she placed it on the bed before taking off her shoes and sliding into something more comfortable. She grabbed the plastic bag and her laptop and plopped on her bed, ready to do her job much better than she'd ever done before, or at least she hoped she would.

Suddenly, her mind wandered to Ash, and she couldn't resist the urge to send him just one message. They had finally exchanged numbers and doing so, proving no further use for the dating site. She brought out her phone and sent him a message:

"Hey."

She added an upside-down smiley face and waited for his reply, looking back at her laptop as she began planning the schedule for the law firm for the coming week. It was seven p.m., and she'd planned the night perfectly; she'd make sure to work on this until ten, and when she was done,

she'd get to proofreading those legal files

Mr. Reynolds had given her.

No breaks.

She repeated under her breath, "No breaks,

Alecia."

But the universe didn't seem to respect her

resolve because immediately after she was

about to start typing, she received a

message. Her heart leaped when she figured

Ash might have replied.

"Hey, Alecia.

Guess what?"

Well, there goes the night's schedule.

"What?"

"I just arrived in town
tonight."

"Really? I thought you
said you'd stay a week?"

"Hmm you don't sound as
excited as I thought you'd be."

"Okay, you caught me, I'm
actually glad you're back.

109

Happy?"

"No, not actually."

"Now you're being more dramatic
than me on that Valentine's Day
night."

He sent a laughing face smiley.

"Oh you were so dramatic." Ash replied

"Let's please not talk about it.
I don't want to facepalm myself.
So, why aren't you happy?

You wanted to stay longer in New Jersey?"

Alecia replied

"No, I'm going back tomorrow."

"Tomorrow?"

"Yeah, I just came today

cuz I didn't have much to do.

I came to see you.

It's been a while."

"You came all the way from

New Jersey just to see me?" Alecia said

smiling to herself

"You're making it sound like a
big deal.
New Jersey isn't that far."

"But that's still a huge thing you did for
me."

"Well, you know what would
make it worth it?
Come visit.
We can go out. I mean, it's a
Friday night."

She stared at the screen and bit her lower
lip. She was really looking forward to
hanging out with Ash tonight, and she

112

couldn't help the cozy feeling in her chest knowing that he'd actually come all the way from New Jersey just for her. But there was tons of work. And she couldn't forget that she also had to go to work tomorrow because the judge, from all the days he could have moved Mr. Reynolds' client's next hearing to, chose a Saturday. So, she'd be working her ass off tomorrow, starting from early in the morning. And she wasn't looking forward to getting into trouble again. That probation thing was scaring her a bit, even though she didn't want to admit it.

Her eyes moved back to Ash's text, and guilt pinched her hard for what she was about to do. She couldn't go out with him. If she decided to leave and spend the night with him, she'd get way too carried away and eventually lose track of time, just like last time. Then she'd be late again and ultimately get into even more severe trouble with Mr. Reynolds.

But his sacrifice...

She shook her head. As he said, it hadn't been a big deal; she tried to convince herself. Her fingers hovered over the keyboard while she contemplated what to type. She was in such a tight spot. What should she do?

She started to vent to the phone screen, "Ash, why do you always have to do these things? Why? You could at least try to be an inconsiderate jerk like Noah for once, can't you? Now, how do I say no? Just how?"

By typing a quick excuse with an apology and tossing the phone away from her like it was about to explode, because that's exactly what she did. She couldn't bear to see his reply.

She just couldn't. She probably sounded so ungrateful, cold, and mean. She sighed. He must have thought she was so full of herself. She decided not to think about it and rather distract herself with work. If she had just rejected a promising and charming offer for this work, she might as well do it. It had literally cost her peace of mind.

About thirty minutes into her ramen-fueled working session, she heard a ring on her doorbell. Ash? That was the first thought that popped into her head. Her heart skipped a beat. Why would Ash actually come to see her? She assumed he was probably offended by the text. So offended that he came in person? With knitted eyebrows, she trod towards the door before

116

waiting to check if the person would eventually leave. When the person knocked again, she took a deep breath and got ready to see Ash. She'd explain why she rejected him so icily and tell him all about the probation thing. She pulled the door open, but the person whose face she was greeted with wasn't Ash's. Instead, it was one that managed to make her sick to her stomach.

"Alecia-"

"What are you doing here?"

Noah looked behind her into the apartment. "I thought I forgot something here. I came to get it."

Of course.

Her blood boiled at his audacity. He hadn't replied to her messages, canceled their plans on Valentine's Day, and was possibly cheating on her, yet here he was, back here only to tell her that he forgot something and wanted to retrieve it. Jerk!

She stepped aside to let him in. If he got everything he owned tonight, then he wouldn't have an excuse to come back here, so she wouldn't have any more reasons to see him again. He walked in and went straight for the closet. She leaned on the wall and watched him with arms crossed against her chest. She watched him search through the closet thoroughly for whatever he needed, wondering if she should inquire about the lady's voice she'd heard. It could be possible that she was just misunderstanding him.

All of a sudden, her old feelings for Noah, which she'd worked so hard to bury, began to resurface. She gathered her courage and decided to call him "Noah?"

"What?" He placed his hands on his waist and scrutinized the closet. "Did you see an orange file in here recently? I can't find it, and it's very important."

She shook her head. "No, I haven't seen such."

He clicked his tongue and continued his search.

"Noah, I want to ask you something," Alecia blurted out again after a while.

"What is it?"

"Noah, who was that girl I heard through your phone on Valentine's Day?"

He looked up, and his expression turned from shock to anger. "What do you mean by that?"

She sighed. "Noah, can you just please answer this question without getting angry. Who was she?" She then decided to go straight to the point. "Are you cheating on me?"

Noah immediately looked away and returned to the closet. Meanwhile, Alecia was left without an answer. She waited

121

patiently for his reply, but he just pulled out an orange file and whispered, "Found it," to himself before walking past her.

She turned around. "Noah? Why are you avoiding my question?"

He let out a sigh of frustration. "You wanna know the answer? Then fine. I wasn't working on Valentine's Day, I was actually with someone."

His words hit her like a blow to the chest, and she pressed her lips into a thin line to stop herself from crying. He hadn't noticed her state, so he continued, "Alecia, she's rich. Her father is super wealthy, and if I manage to get her, who knows what her dad would do for me."

Alecia stared at him in disbelief. "You're cheating on me with her because her dad's rich?"

"Alecia, I'm not cheating on you. Let's face it, our relationship practically ended when I decided to move. We both knew we couldn't do this long-distance thing."

"It's not even that long, Noah. We're like a two-hour drive away from each other!"

He sighed. "Alecia, I can't lose this girl. She's rich, hot. Look, let's just move on already."

"Hot?" she asked, totally ignoring all the other things he'd said. So, this girl was prettier than her?

He took the file and left the apartment, and immediately he did so, Alecia slammed the door on him. What a fucking bastard!

Her anger was burning so much that she had to get a glass of iced water and drink it before cooling down. She couldn't believe how blunt Noah was. He could have at least lied—or sugar-coated. Why'd he have to put her down so much in comparison to his new girlfriend? She held back her tears because she usually didn't fancy crying, but she really had to talk to someone about this before she exploded. She looked at the work materials littered all over her bed and her food. Then, she sighted her phone and hurried to grab it. She could meet up with Ash. He would listen and make her feel better. Talking to him always seemed to give her some kind of peace.

But then, she stopped when she remembered that she had just rejected his offer to take her out tonight. She looked at their messages, and he'd just replied with an "ok". Nothing else.

He was definitely disappointed. What was wrong with her? She considered sending him a message saying that she'd changed her mind, but then, the reality of the amount of work she needed to get done by tomorrow hit her. Mr. Reynolds... he'd told her to be at work early tomorrow, and then, there was the probation. If she went out with Ash tonight, she might as well be forfeiting her job. Disappointed, she dropped the phone again.

Fine! she thought. I'll work tonight. I hope you're happy now, Mr. Reynolds?

She tried to ignore how hurt she felt and Noah's words ringing in her ears, focusing on the schedule she was organizing. Tonight's plan had also been ruined now because of Noah's appearance. She let out a sigh and tried to channel her mind to her laptop. Ash didn't deserve this. He really didn't.

It was already eleven P.M. when her eyelids started getting heavier and heavier. Unconsciously, she remembered how it felt to sleep on Ash's shoulder the other night, and all of a sudden, all she wanted to do was talk to him. Ever since he left, she'd always think back to that moment. It was crazy how just one day with him could have such an effect on her. Even his cologne, she hadn't been able to get the scent out of her head. She reached out for her phone and decided to call him. Even if she couldn't meet him tonight, she could at least hear his voice. Besides, she'd make sure tomorrow night would be all for the both of them. Then, she quickly remembered him telling her that he was going to leave again tomorrow, and her heart sank. She sent him a text instantly:

"When are you coming back? After leaving tomorrow." She asked

She waited for his reply for what seemed like an eternity, but he still hadn't come online. Perhaps she should have just called him. She went back to her work and began proofreading. Her only hope was that he wasn't mad at her for canceling. No, Ash was a mature person. He was probably just disappointed, and plus she did explain her work life to him, so she was sure he'd understand her situation. It took forever, but it finally came, Ash's reply:

"Don't worry, I'll only stay there two days.

129

We'll meet again on Monday."

She smiled at the screen. Of course he understood. He was Ash. In the past, if Alecia had canceled on Noah, he'd ghost her for at least three days. She quickly replied with a "can't wait" and dropped the phone. She finally didn't feel bad while working that night, though she still felt like she could have seen him tonight. It had been a while since she'd seen Ash in person, and these constant texts and calls weren't enough. She loved his company; she couldn't deny that. Later that night, she completed her task and went to bed. However, it wouldn't have made a difference if she'd stayed out late with Ash, because that night, she'd stayed up late thinking of him, wondering why her stupid job was so against the both of them seeing each other.

CHAPTER SIX

"Right there," Alecia told the Bolt driver, pointing to the club Ash had told her to meet him at. It had a bright neon sign spelling out Brands on the front. The driver grinded to a halt in front of the place, and Alecia stepped out. She then brought out her phone and texted Ash that she had arrived. Just as promised, he had come back on Monday, and they both had decided to meet up again. She stood outside, waiting for him for a while before he finally showed up.

"Hey," he said, approaching her.

She smiled back at him and placed both her hands in her jacket pockets. It was still a bit cold. "Hey," she drawled playfully. "So, I'm actually sorry for not coming Saturday night. I actually had a ton of work to do, and my boss has been really strict lately."

He shrugged. "It's okay, though it is weird that we only get to meet up at night."

She shook her head in agreement. "I know, right?"

"You wanna come in?" He asked, pointing behind him to the club.

Alecia nodded. "Yeah, but just so you know, I don't drink."

He grinned. "Don't worry, you don't have to. I just wanted you to meet my friends."

Alecia couldn't control the smile that formed across her face. Ash's friends? She had always wanted to know more about Ash, but he wasn't a very open person. Maybe he was willing to open up to her about his life now. She was just glad their relationship was getting much stronger,

135

even though she wasn't sure what to expect from them—but she was certain she'd like them. In addition to getting to know Ash, this would also give her a chance to socialize with people she probably would actually like, instead of those stuck-up lawyers she was forced to work with and her boss.

"Your friends?" she repeated, tilting her head at him. "Hope they're just as fun as you."

He ran his fingers through his hair. "Well, not too much, but we can work it out."

She laughed. "You're not that special. Stop being so full of yourself."

"Okay then. So, you wanna meet them?"

"Yeah, sure!" He escorted her into the club, and when they got there, she began to look around, watching the group of people who were dancing and having a good time. Alecia knew one thing for sure: she didn't have that much confidence to dance in front of so many people, although she'd always really wanted to do so.

Ash led her to the bar, and she noticed a bunch of people seated there, talking. One was a curly-haired girl, and the rest were two guys.

One of the guys looked up and said as soon as he spotted her, "Hey, Alecia right?"

She nodded. She wondered how he knew her name. "Yeah, that's me."

"Ashley didn't mention you were this pretty," the other girl said, and she beamed.

Ashley? Of course, his name was abbreviated.

"Thanks, you're really pretty too," she complimented meekly.

"Oh stop. I'm Lisa by the way," the girl replied. Ash introduced all of them, and soon, they were all engaged in a long conversation about music, and Alecia also found out the three of them were also army officers. Two of the guys, Natt and Walter, and Lisa. She also noticed something else; Lisa was the only one who called Ash by his full name.

"What do you want, Alecia? Don't worry, it'll be on me. I'm feeling generous today," Lisa said, taking a sip of her drink.

139

"Oh, sorry, I actually don't drink."

Lisa stared at Alecia like she had just said that candy grew on trees.

"You don't drink? Really?"

Was that a problem? Alecia wondered. "Uh, no, I don't. I don't like the taste."

Lisa shrugged. "Well, that's kind of a boring trail if you ask me, but it's okay."

And suddenly, Alecia didn't like Lisa anymore.

"You don't have to be high to prove that you aren't boring," she stated coolly.

Lisa looked at her wide-eyed. "Chill, girl. I was only kidding with you."

Alecia inwardly rolled her eyes while the rest watched the both of them, before Ash decided to change the topic: "So, who's hungry?"

Everyone agreed, and he left to get some pizza. When he came back, Alecia was already talking with Natt. He was pretty interesting, Alecia admitted, as she learned

141

that he was from Seoul and that he had actually left his home without telling anyone, to come to the US. He'd wanted to become a designer, but things had changed. He narrated how he'd gotten recruited to join the army and how his family had found out about everything. They had been mad, but when they saw what he was doing, they'd been extremely proud of him. Alecia listened intently.

"I can't imagine leaving home without telling my parents about it," she said. "They'd kill me if they found me."

Natt laughed. "Eh, they're happy for me now."

"No wonder you joined the army. You're so brave."

He laughed again and took a sip of his drink. "I've been told."

They continued to discuss, but Alecia couldn't help but wonder if Ash had a family. Why hadn't he told her anything about his life? She was intrigued to know, but whenever she'd asked him about himself, he'd just shift the topic back to her. She stared at him at the other side of the bar. He was talking to Lisa, laughing, while she, on the other hand, continuously placed her hand on his arm while doing so. For some inexplicable reason, Alecia wanted to take her hand off of him. She continued to watch them for a while, but then, all of a sudden, Ash's eyes met hers, and her heart skipped a beat. She quickly looked away, picking up a slice of pizza and taking an awkward bite. Why had she been staring at them like that? Of course they could be all close. They're friends!

Soon, she looked in that direction again, but both Ash and Lisa had disappeared. Where had they gone? She scanned the club, but they were nowhere to be found. She was worried now. Where was he? And why'd he have to go with Lisa?

"Where did Ash go?" she asked Natt, and he looked around as well.

"I don't know. I think he went out with Lisa. They are really close."

His words were like a sting to her. Really close? Did they… like each other? Was that why she had been so rude to her earlier? She tried to reassure herself, No, Alecia. Stop! Ash said he didn't have time to meet people and find love. That's why he's on a

145

dating app. If he liked Lisa, he wouldn't have been on a damn dating app!

Soon, the both of them returned, and Alecia felt the need to leave as soon as possible. Maybe she just wanted to get Ash away from Lisa. Was she that toxic? She didn't know.

"Ash," she said in a low voice.

He came closer. "Yeah, what?"

"It's getting late. I told you I can't stay for long. So, please, if you don't mind, can you give me a ride back home?"

146

He agreed without thinking twice. "Sure."

"Thanks," she whispered. She could notice Lisa looking at both of them from the side.

"You're leaving, Ashley?" she asked, and the way she had said the word 'Ashley' pricked Alecia in so many incomprehensible ways.

"Yeah, I'll see you guys later then."

In a few minutes, they were both in Ash's car. Alecia looked at him for a while before asking, "Ash, why don't I visit you at your house?"

"That's random," he commented. "I don't know. Maybe because I've never invited you."

"Well, can I?"

He hesitated. "Well, I don't usually like having people at my house, so…"

She nodded understandingly. She just wanted to know more about him, but she still appreciated him introducing her to his friends. Yet, she still felt interested to know other parts of him, like his family, his childhood, and how he joined the army.

She wanted to know all those other things about him.

"It's okay; you don't have to invite me. We hardly have time to see each other anyway."

He dropped her off at home, and she freshened up before going to bed, happy that she might have lost Noah, but Ash had come to patch that up quickly.

The next day, she had gotten back from work earlier than usual, and since she'd been thinking about Ash all day, she decided to give him a call. Work had been less lately. Maybe Mr. Reynolds realized

149

that she needed a break, and instead of giving her one, he'd decided to reduce her workload. It was just as good too. She was glad because, at least, she didn't have to work till she got bags under her eyes—and she still did get paid well. So, it also proved that her boss still had a conscience at least.

Ash's phone rang, and Alecia waited patiently for him to answer, while unpacking the to-go cappuccino she'd bought from Cherub Cafés on her way home. The phone continued to ring for a while, then it unexpectedly disconnected. She stared at the phone blankly and dialed his number again. Still no answer. She didn't give up, calling him for a third time, and to her relief, he answered.

"Hello," she said.

"What?"

She was stunned by his reply. "Uh, just wanted to check up on you."

"I'm good. Anything else?"

Her forehead scrunched. "Um-"

He hung up.

Weird. What had that been all about? She tried calling him again to ask about his sudden demeanor. He picked up almost immediately. "What is it?"

"What's up? Are you mad because of something?"

She heard him sigh through the phone. "Look, Alecia, for one sec, can you leave me alone?"

Her mouth hung open. "Leave you alone?"

"I'm not in the mood for this right now." Then, he cut the call again.

152

What was up with him? Pissed, she went to their chats, and when she found out he was currently online, she sent him a text:

"What's up with you?"

She noticed he had read the message, but he didn't reply, and immediately, he went ahead to go offline. Why was he acting this way out of nowhere? Had she done something last night? Was it Lisa? There was something familiar about this situation. Then, she realized it. This wasn't a deja vu, this was the exact same way Noah had acted before he'd begun ghosting her.

Alecia became worried. Did that mean Ash
was going to ghost her as well? She sent
him another message:

"Ash?
You're acting really rude right now.
Did I do something last night?
Reply so I can know what the matter is."

This was dumb! She sounded so desperate.
But he was the one with the abruptness! He
was the one acting up! Her heart leaped
when she noticed he'd come online and
read all her messages, but he didn't reply to
them. Irritated, she decided to sleep,
waking up at intervals to check if he'd

replied, but no, he was still online but hadn't replied to any of her messages!

He had literally been on his phone all night and still no reply. Her mind began to overthink the situation. His friends might probably have told him that they didn't like her, and so he decided to ghost her to please them.

She frowned at the thought and turned to the other side of her bed. Stupid Ash. She looked at her phone again, and he was still online but hadn't replied. She dropped it. What if Lisa had told him to do this? Natt's words replayed in her head: The both of them are really close. She was sure it was her. She sighed and closed her eyes to get some sleep. Guys were all alike. They got bored easily and ghosted you as soon as they did so. Then, they would start acting like it was all your fault. And here she was, fretting over one of them.

It was probably two in the morning when she woke up. She sat up on her bed to check her phone again, and when she saw he'd actually replied, she rushed to check what he'd said. She was expecting an apology or an explanation for his rude attitude at least, but what she saw instead made her blood boil.

"Alecia, just go to bed."

She scowled at the message. Who did this guy think he was? Her fingers began to type furiously on the keyboard, causing the sound of thumbs hitting her phone screen to echo throughout the room, but then, she realized he'd probably just ignored this message as well, so there would be no point in expressing how she was feeling to him. Besides, it was her concern that fueled his attitude, so she deleted the paragraph she was about to send and went ahead to take a deep breath... and delete his number.

That'll do. No more Ash.

She knew it was a big step, but she didn't care. She didn't want history to repeat with

Ash this time in place of Noah. She laid back on her bed and closed her eyes to fall asleep. Of course, what was she expecting? Those damn dating apps never work.

CHAPTER SEVEN

Most times, when people go through a heartbreak, it usually takes them a while to move on. But Alecia thought that unique people like her got interested in someone new the next day, then got their hearts broken again a few days later. That was the summary of the past two weeks of her life. The loss of contact between Ash and her hadn't seemed to affect him at all, but it sure did affect her. And it was the kind of effect where one decided they didn't deserve this and chose to take care of themselves, sparing not a single thought for him. But they'd find themselves thinking about him every chance they got to get lost in their minds.

So, she was going to make sure she wouldn't let Ash cross her mind. And how did she plan on doing that? By working like her life depended on it, earning her side eyes from the people at her workplace.

"Mr. Reynolds, I've sent you the files you asked for," she told her boss, but he held up his hands, telling her to wait. She then realized he was on a call.

When he was done, he looked at her.

"What?"

"I've sent you the files, Sir," she told him.

He looked into his phone, and she stood, waiting for what he'd say. He looked at her, raising a brow. "And what about the one for Mr. Fredrick's case?"

She pointed to his phone. "I also sent it. Check your messages."

He averted his gaze from her to his phone and scrolled through. When he found it, he glanced at her for a second before walking

161

away. She smirked to herself. Guess someone doesn't have something to complain about today, she said to herself. She moved back to her desk and continued with her activities when she heard her phone beep. She just got a text. Wondering who it was, she took a look at her phone only to see a "hey" from an unknown number. She didn't usually reply to unknown numbers, and so she didn't acknowledge the message. But a thought quickly crossed her mind: what if the texter was Ash? She stared at the message. Well, what if it was? He was probably bored now and had decided to send her a message. She carried on with her work, though her hand

162

twitched to respond to the message. It could be someone else for all she knew. She picked up the phone and sent a reply:

"Hello."

Then, before she could continue with her work, another text came in:

"Alecia, can we talk?"

Oh, it was definitely Ash. She kept her phone aside and faced her laptop. Deep down, she'd known it had been Ash all along. She'd just wanted to talk to him—or at least check if he'd wanted to talk to her.

"What do you want now, Ash?" she muttered. After all this time, he'd finally buried his dumb ego and decided to talk to her. Lisa had probably rejected him, so he was looking for some comfort in her. She shook her head. What was she thinking? Lisa was just his friend.

In fact, she didn't know what to believe right now. I was supposed to be focusing on myself, remember? She thought. There was no time for Ash or any mental stress that comes with it.

Heaven knew how many times she'd wondered what the heck she had done to deserve such a sour temperament from him that day. She looked at her phone again when another message beeped in:

"I'm really sorry for how I spoke to you that night. Just, please reply and let's talk about it." Ash sent

He'd made her restless when he hadn't replied, and she was going to do the same. She ignored him all day till her shift was over. She walked out of the premises and ordered a ride to the supermarket. She kept looking at her phone, but he still hadn't sent any more messages. Was she being childish and seeking attention? No, she had all the right to act this way. She browsed through the items in the supermarket and selected everything she needed. Part of 'focusing on herself' was improving her diet and putting an end to wasting money on take-outs and staking up the boxes and plastic bags in her trash can. She was going to buy actual groceries today, and she was going to make an actual meal today. Exciting.

A new message suddenly came in:

"Alecia?"

She was done buying everything she needed, and she stood in line to pay for them. When it was her turn, the lady told her the price, and she paid her before taking everything and leaving. Her apartment wasn't far from there, so she chose to walk. As she trekked, in front of her was a guy resting his arm around a girl's neck and pulling her close. She rolled her eyes and took out her phone to use it as a clutch to avoid looking at them get all syrupy in front of her. She was pretty sure he was just going to get tired of her someday and totally ice her out for his 'friend' or for a girl with a rich Dad. She wondered what Noah was doing now with his new target. She searched for his Instagram. Noah didn't post much on the app, but since she'd blocked him on all other social media platforms, she had nowhere else to assess him from, so she was hoping to find something useful there.

And she found something more than useful.

Beach photos, penthouse cuddles, a fucking highlight just for her! Her hands curled into fists. He'd gotten the life he'd wanted. He'd finally got it! Fucking lazy ass! Her eyes began to water as she scrolled through the pictures. She hoped no one around saw her and assumed she was some kind of psycho stalking an innocent couple. She took a deep breath to prevent the tears from dropping.

Alecia, you're a queen. You're a fucking queen. You don't need to be crying over that clown! You're much prettier than his new flat-assed girlfriend! Her subconscious was right. She blinked back tears and looked around to ensure no one had seen her crying. She wasn't paranoid, it was the street lights here. They were capable of powering an entire solar system. As she scanned the area, her eyes stopped at the girl in front of her, and she watched as she looked up at the guy she was with and dropped a kiss on his lips.

Oh for goodness sake, get a room!

She walked past both of them and hurried towards her apartment. Wasn't Valentine's Day last week or two weeks ago? Some people just didn't get enough, did they?

Alecia's heart was broken, she was so confused. Maybe she had actually liked Ash. She sighed. It wasn't fair! Who gets two heartbreaks in less than a month?

Speaking of the devil, she immediately received another text from Ash:

"Alecia, I'm sorry.
Please just talk to me."

When she still didn't say anything, he typed:

"I'm going to come over."

Now, this text startled her. She didn't want to see him right now, and if he came over, he was going to see how much his behavior had affected her—and that was the last thing she wanted him to see.

171

"No, you don't have to."

"So you're ready to talk?"

She waited for a while, thinking.

"What is it you wanna talk about?"

"I want to apologize for the night
I was so rude to you."

"And you took this long to realize
what you did?"

"Something came up that day."

"I'm still waiting for a legit
explanation…"

"Some real crappy stuff happened
to me that day and I took it out
on you. I'm sorry."

"What you did wasn't cool, Ash."

"I know, I know.
That's why I'm apologizing to
you right now.
So, do you forgive me?"

"Ash, it isn't that easy.

Tell me what happened to you.

What was so bad that you totally

lost your cool?"

"Let's meet up and I'll explain

everything.

Sound good?

How about at your apartment?"

"Why not at your house?"

"Alecia."

"Fine, you can come over." She finally

agreed.

She dropped her phone and headed to her apartment. When she got there, she started putting away the things she'd bought. She tried so hard to deny the fact that she was a bit giddy that Ash was coming over, but she shouldn't be. She shouldn't be so forgiving; people would take advantage of her—her dad's words. He'd always been a bit cynical, and maybe she'd gotten just a tinge of that trait.

When she was done, she waited for Ash for a while, but her stomach started to growl, so she decided to make a sandwich while she waited. But, just as she was about to start, the doorbell rang. On opening the door, she spotted a pair of green colored

175

eyes staring right back at her. Ash's hair was now more arranged. And she couldn't ignore his nice physique. It was as if he'd become even more attractive since the last time they met. She tried not to swoon over him and maintained a cool expression.

"So, what did you want to say?" she demanded.

"Aren't you gonna let me in first?"

She stood for a bit before moving aside and letting him walk in. He turned around to face her as she closed the door. She stared back at him expectantly.

176

"So, you're probably wondering why I was so rude to you that day," he began.

"Well, yeah. You made me think I did something wrong, and then you waited until today to apologize."

"I was just stressed out. A lot of shit happened, and I guess I took it out on you that day. I'm sorry."

She looked away with her hands folded. Now she was starting to feel kind of childish. "Well, you could have told me. You're not really open about yourself."

He quirked a brow. "What do you mean?"

"I mean," she started. "You don't tell me about all the things you're up to, and I've never been to your house. Also that Lisa-" She stopped mid-sentence. "I mean, your friend, Lisa, we didn't seem to get along much, and I was assuming it was because of her you ghosted me."

He stared at her, confused, and she added, "Because you know, you two are all close and all…"

He creased his forehead. "Alecia, you know I won't just ice someone out just because my friends told me to."

Her voice was lower now. "But you didn't give me a reason."

"Look, I'm here now. Okay? And I'm ready to make it up to you."

The sincerity in his voice forced her to forgive him already. But she wouldn't let him know that. "Okay then. Can you cook?"

He nodded. "Yeah, I can."

She looked back at the kitchen, then at him. "If you make something really good for me, then I'll forgive you."

He smirked. "That's it? Cook? I'll have you know that if I hadn't been recruited into the army, I'd have been a chef." He walked into the kitchen and looked around.

"Oh really?" She feigned disbelief.

He turned back and stared at her with those trademark charming eyes. "You know you're really taking advantage of me."

She couldn't help laughing. "I was too exhausted to cook. But don't worry; I'll help." She walked over to him and watched as he slid a knife out and sliced some meat like a professional.

"What are you making?" She asked, curious.

"I don't know…" He raised the meat and studied it before placing it on the chopping board again and poking holes into it. "Probably chicken pot pie."

"Chicken what? Tonight?" She panicked. "Ash, you're gonna use up all my ingredients!"

181

He pointed the knife at her. "You said I should make something really good. What were you expecting? A sandwich?"

A smile tugged at her lips. "But-"

He rolled his eyes. "Now, would you please cut the vegetables, Alecia?"

She kept watching him. She would definitely kill to have this guy in her kitchen every day looking this handsome.

He snapped her out of her thoughts. "Now, are you going to keep watching me? '

182

Because I can do this with or without your help."

"Fine, I'm going to help." Raising her hands in defeat, she took out the vegetables and started cutting them. How did this guy manage to win her over every time? How had he made her forgive him so easily? Dad, I'm sorry, but you'd also keep up that rule until you meet this Ash guy, she thought. I promise I'll be cynical next time.

CHAPTER EIGHT

"Kane," Ash replied, loosening the braids on Alecia's hair. After Ash was done making the dish, he suggested he stay a while and talk.

Alecia sat on the floor of her room, taking a bite of what Ash had made, and she wasn't even going to lie, but it was probably one of the best chicken pot pies she'd ever had—and she'd had many.

"So, you're Ashley Kane?" she said. "Hmm, doesn't sound bad." She looked up at him. "Can I ask you one more thing?"

"That's enough questions for today, Alecia."

"Please."

"No."

She narrowed her eyes on him. "You're so annoying."

He chuckled, and that simple gesture tugged at something in Alecia's chest. She loved hearing him laugh, she couldn't deny

186

it. "Okay, why don't we go on a date tomorrow?"

"And?"

"And I'll answer everything. But now, I'll have to get going. It's late."

She pouted. "Oh, can't you just stay the night?"

He was now done loosening up her braids and placed both hands on the sides of her head from behind. "I wish I could, but I've got a lot of things to do tonight."

She frowned. Things.

"But don't worry. Tomorrow's date will make up for it."

"Where are we going?" She rested on his knee.

He scratched the back of his head. "Haven't thought of it yet. But, just be ready."

It was as if a piece of Alecia had left with Ash when he'd walked through her apartment door and to the hallway. She watched him as he left, and when she got back inside, she started from that moment to plan her outfit. She didn't have many options; however, she was sure there was at least something appropriate. A little more information about where we're going would have helped, Ash! She selected a dress—no jeans—no, what if it were a classy restaurant?

"Ugh! What do I wear?!" She rummaged through her closet for almost half of the night, and it was as if after all her hard work, she'd ended up with the most ridiculously looking outfit in the history of fashion. Ash had a great fashion sense, she noticed. So, she didn't want to make him look bad by looking bad, if that made

189

sense. She couldn't imagine him showing up with one of his fancy coats, and she walked up to him looking like a hobo. She shook her head, feeling more resolved. She'd definitely look good tomorrow night. Definitely!

Her closet was magical, really. Just as soon as she'd decided to wear something perfect, the expensive evening dress her dad had gotten her when he hadn't known prom dresses weren't in fact cocktail dresses appeared. It had been costly, but he hadn't been able to take it back as the store had a 'no return' policy. She'd ended up wearing a much cheaper one to prom that year.

Nevertheless, she'd kept the first dress with her just in case, but over time, she'd thought she'd lost it. But, there it was now—in her closet. She wondered how.

Ash's car pulled up in front of her apartment building, and the same old lady from the Valentine's Day night saw Alecia again, walking over to a car in a pretty dress. She gave her a mischievous smirk as she examined her appearance. Alecia blushed, avoiding her gaze. Why'd she always have to appear when she was going on a date with Ash? Who knew if he even liked her? Suddenly, she became worried when the realization hit her. Ash might not like her. He might have only been seeing her as a friend this whole time!

But it's not a worry, she only saw him as a friend too, right?

She clutched her purse tightly and walked towards his car. He grinned at her from the driver's seat, and trepidation didn't even let her return it with a decent smile. She and Ash were friends, right? Or probably more than that? She got into the passenger's seat, and her skin felt warm from his gaze. How could she say he was just a friend when he made her feel like this?

"You look so different today," he said.

"In a good way or bad way?"

He faced forward again. "Definitely in a good way."

She smiled. "Thanks. It's nothing much."

If only "nothing much" meant the most expensive dress she owned, a YouTube make-up tutorial, and hours and hours of styling and restyling her hair.

As they drove to the restaurant, she noticed there was something different today. She felt there was more tension between the both of them, and she was acting a trifle more anxious than she usually did. She glanced at the stunningly looking guy in the driver's seat and wondered if he felt it too. They got to the destination, and she realized she was right. It was a fancy Italian restaurant. She was glad she hadn't ended up wearing those jeans. Ash opened the door for her and reached out his hand to her. "Shall we?"

"I see you had the whole day to read chivalry books," she commented, and his face brightened up into a laugh.

"Oh my goodness, Alecia. Do you have to attack me every single time?"

Smiling, she accepted his hand. They both proceeded into the restaurant and took a seat. The waiter came to take their order. "What would you two have today?"

Alecia stared at the menu. "Um, well…"

"Oh, she didn't come here for the food. She's actually on a mission to outdress everyone else," Ash said. Her lips formed into a silly smile, which she tried so hard to cover up with her hand.

"Please, ignore him," she told the waiter.

"I'll just have tacos."

"What about you, señor?"

Ash replied, "Whatever she's having."

The moment the waiter left, she shot a look at Ash. "Really?"

He shrugged. "What?"

"For a soldier, you can be really unserious."

"There isn't a rule that says soldiers can't be funny… or compliment pretty girls," he added, and she blushed.

"Do you really have to do it in front of the waiter?"

"Just letting him know you're the prettiest in the room."

Don't blush, Alecia. Don't blush!

Did she look that pretty? She looked at all the ravishing ladies in the room. Nah, Ash had just been trying to flatter her. Their food arrived soon, and they talked. Ash made her laugh so much, she almost choked on her food. Other times, he maintained eye contact with her that she forgot how to breathe.

Ash took her back to his car, and she assumed he was taking her back home, but she started to become worried when he went in the opposite direction.

"Ash, are we going somewhere else?"

"Didn't you always want to visit my place?"

She beamed. "You're actually taking me to your house?"

198

"It's against my better judgment, but sure."

When she got to Ash's house, it looked pretty from the outside. As she walked towards it, her feet twisted in her heels, and she almost fell, but Ash grabbed her waist just in time. His fingers brushed it slightly before letting go, and to be honest, she wanted to take his hands and place them right back there. Ash hadn't touched her on her waist before today. She wondered why he was so distant. Most guys acted like creeps when they were with girls, but this particular guy she wanted to get close to didn't want to.

Ash led her into his house, and he saw how impressed Alecia was. He didn't understand why, because he hadn't put so much work into it. But he'd put enough, so he didn't want anyone coming in and ruining his sanctuary. Except Alecia. Somehow, he felt Alecia deserved to visit his house. If it wasn't the numerous times he'd come to her house before or the fact that she was the first number on his speed dial, then he probably wouldn't have considered it was only right to bring her here.

Alecia, on the other hand, took the place in. It was so organized—made hers look like a playground. Everything was neat, organized, and the furniture was sleek. The house was so glassy and immaculate that she was scared walking over it would break it.

"Your house is so nice," she said, looking around the place. It also had a comfortable aura to it; the heater was on, and the warmth reminded her of spending Christmas at her dad's. It must be the reason Ash hadn't wanted people coming over—it would ruin his peace and quiet.

"Thanks. You want a drink?"

"Sure."

Ash went into the kitchen, and she trailed behind him before taking a seat on the kitchen counter. He took off his coat, and she watched how his muscles flexed as he opened the fridge and grabbed a jug of orange juice. "You don't drink alcohol, right?"

She snapped out of gawking at him. "Um, yes."

He poured out a glass of the juice and handed it to her. She took small sips, still observing him as he selected a drink for himself. She wondered how it would feel like to kiss him. She wasn't sure if she should be thinking these thoughts, but damn… what she'd do to make him feel the same way about her.

"Are you done?" Ash asked, gesturing to her orange juice.

"Yeah, I'm done." She yanked it out to him, but before he could collect it, it had already spilled on the floor.

"Oh, I'm so sorry."

"It's okay. I'll clean it." He turned back to get a towel.

"No, you don't have to. I'll do it myself." She stood and hurried to take the towel from him, but he turned around and they bumped into each other. He hissed, and she looked up at him, rubbing her forehead. He was so close to her now, and she wasn't sure if she was breathing properly. She figured it out now. Ash! He was the reason she kept blundering.

"Oh, sorry, I don't know why I'm being so clumsy today." Alecia said

"It's okay."

He bent down to clean it, and she joined him. "Here, let me do it."

They bickered on who was going to clean and who was not for a while before Alecia looked up, only to notice his face was just inches away from hers now. Ash looked at her as if trying to discern something. He knew she had recently gone through a breakup, so he stayed a safe distance from her, but how could he keep doing that when she looked at him like that?
And when she looked so breathtaking?

Alecia contemplated if she should lean in and kiss him. He was so up close, and those thoughts were the only thing running through her head. Are you silly, Alecia? she told herself. He probably isn't even thinking of—

Her subconscious was cut short by Ash's lips capturing hers in a kiss, catching her off guard. She was taken aback by his behavior—and also very, very glad. Who knew Ash felt the same way? Tentatively, she lifted up her hands and placed them around his neck. He deepened the kiss and pushed her back, keeping one hand on her waist and the other one on the floor to support himself. He trailed the kiss down to her neck, and she pushed her head back to grant him full access. His fingers reached down to cup her boobs, then down to grab her leg and pull her closer.

"Why do you look so fucking hot today?" he whispered into her left ear, and his hot breath fanning her earlobe coaxed a shiver out of her. His fingers found the hem of her dress, and he caressed her on her inner thigh before she pulled his face back to hers to kiss him. His tongue found its way into her mouth, and when his hand began to stroke her sensitive spot, it was as if electricity ran through her entire body, and she writhed. Noah hadn't been this good; always looking to please himself without considering her. He hadn't been able to drive her crazy with just one touch.

"Ash," she moaned out his name between kisses.

He stopped and responded, "What is it, sweetheart?"

She tried to catch her breath. "What about the orange juice?"

He looked at the orange juice and back at her, a smirk forming on his lips. "I'll deal with it later."

He grabbed the back of her head and kissed her, and then, before she knew it, the zipper of her dress was coming undone. She leaned in closer to him. Then, she ran her fingers through his hair the moment he began to undo the hooks of her bra. He slowly peeled the dress from her body, and when he was about to do the same for the bra, Alecia hesitated. "Can we go to your room first?"

It was his turn to hesitate.

209

But it didn't take long. He quickly stood up, holding her close to him. Without a word, he lifted her and placed her on the kitchen counter. "I think I prefer having you in here."

Her cheeks burned. He grabbed her legs, spread them, and pulled her closer to him. She couldn't seem to tear her eyes away from his. His lips moved from her neck, going lower, and she threw her head back, closing her eyes shut. His hands grabbed her ass and pulled her even closer to him, like they weren't close enough already. She hadn't expected to end up half naked on

Ash's kitchen counter tonight, but surprises happened, didn't they? He ran his hands over her bare waist, and his breath hitched. "You're even hotter than I expected."

When he was done worshiping her body, he carried her to his couch, and she wondered why he was avoiding taking her to his bedroom. But her brain was too hazy from the scent of his cologne to comprehend it. It was cold outside, but the warmth from Ash's body was just what she needed. She laid on his bare chest with his muscular arm wrapped around her, while she got lost in his perfect eyes.

"Why do you keep looking at me like that?" he asked.

"I like your eyes."

"I like your full lips," he said with a husky voice, and her heart skipped a beat. He then went ahead to brush his thumb over it, and she grinned. He was also obsessed with something about her. She then laid on his chest and began to play with his fingers. Ash was so much better than Noah. She was considering telling him that, but before she knew it, she fell asleep on his hard, yet comforting chest.

CHAPTER NINE

Sundays were usually Alecia's most awaited days. Why? Because her boss had no right calling her to work on that day—and now, there was a new reason: Ash. She'd get to spend the whole day with him without getting worried about staying out too late. She was awakened by the smell of coffee— and scones. She opened her eyes slowly and noticed a blanket over her, while she wasn't wearing anything underneath. She sat up, holding the blanket to her chest when she spotted Ash walking over to her with a cup of coffee.

"Here." He handed her the piping hot
coffee.

"Did you also make scones?" she asked.

He nodded.

Well, he hadn't been wrong when he'd said
he was a good chef. It smelled promising.
She narrowed her eyes at him. This guy was
way too charming for his own good.
Breakfast in bed—couch, actually. Heaven
only knew what he was going to do next.

"Charming much?" He flashed her a smug smile.

She took a sip of her coffee. "Very much. You're now making me feel useless."

And by 'useless,' she meant spoiled. Noah had never woken up first just to prepare breakfast for her after a make-out session the night before. In fact, she felt she should be the one doing it. She totally deserved it.

"Don't worry, you can make the next meal," he said, and she smiled, sipping her coffee, careful not to burn her lips—those lips Ash admired so much.

"And when will that be?" she asked.

"Probably not today. I won't be around the whole day."

"Really?"

He took a seat and ruffled her hair. "Yeah, but I'll be back tomorrow."

She pressed her lips into a thin line. "You're always so busy."

"I can say the same about you."

He was giving Alecia a taste of her own medicine. Gosh, it was so disappointing when work had to keep someone away from you. She looked up at him. "Touché. You can go."

She was mostly disappointed by the fact that she had to go back home, just when she was getting so snug at his house. He dropped her off at home, and she bid him goodbye before walking in. She plopped on her bed and smiled to herself. Noah might have found someone new, but she'd also found someone—and this time, he was better than him in every way possible; mentally and physically. She remembered the unappealing pictures of Noah's new girlfriend and scoffed.

The next day, at work, Mr. Reynolds called her to see him in his office. She walked over tentatively and sat opposite him. "Sir, you wanted to see me."

"Yes, I did," he said, going through his phone.

She waited expectantly. "Well, then, what do you want to tell me?"

He didn't look up from his phone. "Yeah, actually, I wanted to talk to you…"

218

He trailed off, and Alecia waited impatiently. He was wasting her time. She needed to get back to work. Yet, he'd be the one complaining that she didn't get enough work done. "Sir?"

"Give me a sec."

Annoyed, she waited.

"Okay." He looked up at her, finally. "I wanted to lift your probation."

"Really, sir?" she asked, surprised.

"Well, apparently, it turns out you've been doing great work lately," he said. "And I recently discovered that you're the least person who gets a leave, so I thought I should grant you one."

She beamed. "Oh my God, sir. Thanks so much!"

"It starts tomorrow. You can wrap up everything you have to do today."

"Sure."

The rest of the day, she completed everything she had to do, causing her to leave the law firm by ten P.M. Mr. Reynolds said he'd give her a one-week break as he wouldn't be able to give anything more than that, and she'd be lying if she said she wasn't still happy with his decision. As long as she got to spend late nights with Ash without fretting over her punctuality, even for a little while, she didn't mind. The next day, she texted Ash:

"Hey, Ash.

I was thinking we should meet up. You decide where, you're really good at that. But it's okay if you're busy."

She hit send on the last message and waited for his reply. It didn't come anytime soon, so she assumed he was just busy. Soon, she got a message from him:

"I am."

Just that? Weird. She sent another message.

"Soo when will you be free?"

"Tonight."

His texts were oddly brief, but she didn't send any further messages. She went to her fridge and looked for the bag of chips she swore she'd seen recently. She rummaged through the fridge and eventually found a bag of marshmallows instead. That would have to do. She took it, poured it out into a bowl, and laid on her bed on her stomach. Then she placed her laptop in front of her and turned on her Netflix. She selected a series and suddenly, she'd found what to do for the rest of her break. Having no idea what people were watching currently, she decided to watch whatever Netflix suggested to her.

Her whole day was spent in laxity as she waited to meet up with Ash that night. She was hoping they could go to his house. Perhaps she could complete the series she was watching with him. She wondered if he even liked movies. He'd never told her. Maybe they could just make out like they did last time, and this time, she was completely prepared for it. She bit her nails as she recalled that night. Ash really liked her, she was sure of it now. Later that night, she sent him another message. She knew she was being clingy, but he was the one person she could be herself around.

"Are you free yet? There's something I wanna do with you." She said.

"I'm actually tired. Not in the mood." Ash replied

224

She frowned at her phone screen. He was 'not in the mood'? Was she supposed to be offended by that? No, she was guessing he was just having another bad day.

"What happened? Did something piss you off?" Alecia asked

He read her message but didn't reply.

"Not again," she said to herself. She was certain this guy had a serious case of bipolar disorder. One second, he's all romantic and charming, the next, he's cold and distant. She wasn't going to send him another

225

message. She'd wait for his reply. Though, he had told her last time that he had some problems, and he only took it out on her. But he'd also promised her he wouldn't do that again. What was wrong with him? She dialed his number and gave him a call, but he didn't answer, and when she tried the second time, he rejected the call.

"Ash, why do you continuously do this?" she asked herself and tossed her phone to the side, hoping that he'd call back soon.

He hadn't called back last night and the rest of the day as well, so she figured she should go to his house and check up on him. She'd admit that she was mad, but she was still a bit worried. What if he was going through something right now, and he wasn't open enough to tell her about it? Her ride stopped in front of Ash's house, and she came down and walked to his front door. Ash didn't like people coming over, especially unannounced, but she didn't care. Taking a deep breath, she raised her index finger to press the doorbell, but before she did so, someone already opened it, and she was shocked to see Natt.

"Hey, Alecia. Ash didn't say you were joining us," he said, surprised.

"Joining you?" she creased her forehead.

He nodded, and she noticed a drink in his hand. It looked like one of those alcoholic drinks she'd seen her dad drinking. But then again, it could just be apple juice. "Yeah, the rest are inside."

She waved off what he'd said and moved to her main reason for coming here. "Where's Ash?"

He pointed back. "He's inside."

"Is he okay?"

Natt shook his head. "Should he not be?"

"No, it's just..."

"We're having a barbeque."

She stared at him in disbelief. "A barbeque?"

Ash had been ignoring her, and she had been worried sick that something might have happened to him, but he was having the time of his life. He was having a freaking barbeque? She didn't get this man.

229

"He's in there right now?" she asked, and Natt nodded cautiously.

"Yeah…? He's with Lisa. Should I go call him?"

Of course, he'd make time for Lisa, but he wouldn't even reply to her messages. She could feel her anger burn to the tip of her fingers as she clutched her phone tightly and turned back, walking away. Ash didn't like her. If he did, he wouldn't act this way. But what about that night? Ugh! She stormed to the road and kept walking on the sidewalk. She tried to order a cab, but the internet service in these streets could make a grown man cry. She groaned and slid it back into her pocket. She hadn't seen a single taxi driver pass her since she started walking, and she couldn't imagine herself walking forty-five minutes to her house. What was wrong with New York City today? She sighed. But what else could she do? Her hands were in her coat pockets as she sped up her walking pace. Her phone suddenly rang, and her heart almost stopped when she assumed it might be Ash calling. Natt probably informed him about her visit. She looked at the number, and for goodness sake, it was just Damien, a damned coworker.

"Hello," she managed to say through gritted teeth. She calmed herself down and repeated, "Hello?"

"Yes, um, I'm sorry to disturb you, but where did you leave Miss Hannah's case's file?"

"I gave it to Mr. Montez! I told you all this before I left!" she almost yelled.

He stayed quiet on the other line for a while. "Oh, that's right. I'll ask him."

She hung up. Now, she was the one venting on an innocent person. She took a deep, cold breath. It was particularly colder tonight. Something light and cold fell on her nose, and she raised her hand to feel it, only to find out it was snow. It was the end of February; winter should be over by now. But that was just how it was in New York City. The winters refused to end. Though, it was sort of a good thing. She was hoping the snow would ruin Ash's stupid barbeque. She felt like an ice pop when she reached her apartment, and so, she decided to spoil herself with a hot shower. When she was done, she left the bathroom and turned on her phone to check if Ash had tried to reach out to her, but no, nothing. She got nothing! She put on her pajamas and took out her laptop to complete her series, but this time, angrily. In fact, she wasn't even angry anymore, she was utterly confused! What had she even done this time? She was sure she hadn't done anything. Ash was just very inconsistent, and unpredictable—in both positive and negative ways.

Her mind didn't assimilate what was going on in the movie as she constantly kept checking her phone. Fed up, she decided to call him herself. His phone rang, and much to her surprise, he picked it up.

"Hello, Ash."

"Alecia."

"You didn't reply to my texts or answer my calls. What's wrong?"

"Sorry, I've just been busy."

"Busy having a barbeque?"

"You came?"

"Didn't Natt tell you?"

"Well, Natt isn't around, so..."

She needed to talk to Ash about this bipolar thing. "Ash, can we meet tomorrow?"

He sighed. "Sorry, I can't tomorrow."

Of course.

"Well then, when can we meet?"

"I don't really know. Uh… I'll text you when I decide."

"Hello?" He hung up the call. For the love of God! What kind of a demeanor did this Ash guy have? She turned off her laptop. She was in no mood to watch anything

236

right now. She sighed, trying not to let herself cry. This was all her fault. She'd forgiven him last time, and so he hadn't seen a problem making the same mistake again. Maybe he just didn't like her that way. She was probably just that friend he takes on dates and invites to his house to mess around with. She facepalmed herself. She had no idea what Ash wanted from her, or how he pegged her as in his life. And silly her, she went ahead to pin all her dumb expectations on him, only for him to give her high hopes and crush them when the time was right for him.

CHAPTER TEN

Alecia was beginning to think that maybe she shouldn't have been so distant with people before because, yes, she was used to being very content in her own company, but after Noah had left her and Ash came along to make her feel better, she'd been craving other people's company more. Especially Ash's.

Natt was a good friend who didn't ghost her, and they chatted a lot recently, but she didn't want to spend too much time with a friend of Ash's right in front of him. She was considerate like that.

But it might not even matter because Ash's feelings for her weren't looking mutual.

"Kachi, how are you?" her Dad said through the phone. That was the name her Dad preferred calling her. It was a native Nigerian name.

"I'm good. I'm currently on a break from work," she replied.

"Okay, and how is Noah?"

She clucked her tongue. She'd forgotten to tell her Dad about their break up. He'd

240

really liked Noah a lot, she didn't know if he'd take it.

"Dad, actually…"

"Uh oh. What is it?"

She sighed. "Actually, Noah and I… kind of… broke up."

"Broke up? Why? You kids are always quick to part ways whenever someone does something trivial. You know quarrels are a part of every relationship, right?"

"No, Dad," she said. "We didn't quarrel. It's not what you're thinking."

"Then what went wrong? You two looked so good together—did that boy hurt you?" His voice was now sounding more worried.

"Dad, stop assuming things," she replied. "He just cheated on me."

"He cheated?"

"Yes, and with some stupid girl that has a rich Dad 'cuz he wants an easy life," she said with a frown.

"Well, darling, that is what you call a lazy ass. He can't even work for himself."

She laughed because that was what she also called him.

"But jokes aside, dear, are you okay?" he asked, concern filling his voice.

She nodded, even though he couldn't see her. "I actually got over it quicker than you think."

"Are you sure? I can come over if you want to."

"No, Dad. You don't have to. I actually met a new guy immediately after the betrayal. He was great. His name is Ash."

"Ash?" He said the name plainly. "What kind of a name is that?"

She laughed. "That's what I thought."

"Is Ash a nice man? Does he have a job?" Her Dad had already begun the interrogation.

She replied, "He's nice-" most of the time "-and he's a soldier."

"Wow, that's great!"

"—but Dad, I don't know if he feels the same way about me. I don't know if he likes me as well. He keeps giving me mixed emotions, and I can't make out what he's thinking."

"Kachi, just go and ask him."

"I don't know. What if he rejects me?"

"Then, that's that," he stated. "If he actually likes you, he wouldn't want to lose you. But if he doesn't, then you'll just have to move on. He won't give you a good answer."

She considered what her Dad was saying, but she was too dreary of Ash's reply to go on with the idea. People said rejection was much more painful than getting physically hurt—even deep cuts!—and she was not in the state of mind to bear that kind of pain. She'd rather just hold on to the hope that he liked her back deep down in his heart, even if she didn't get that direct answer from him. The way he looked at her and the way he'd made such an effort to gain her forgiveness the other day was all she needed to convince her he also liked her and prevent any heartbreaks. The last thing she needed right now was to hear Ash reject her with his own words. She wouldn't be able to take it.

She also sometimes asked herself if Ash was aware of her feelings for him because if he was, he wouldn't be acting this way— unless he was an inconsiderate person. Her phone beeped, and she picked it up. It was a message from Ash. She hated herself for being so excited about it.

"Hey."

She didn't want to be juvenile this time. She didn't want this unnecessary tension between the both of them to drag any further. She wanted them to sort things out. If Ash had a problem, he should talk to her about it. She was more than willing to hear him out. Besides, he was the one who'd listened to her rant on and on about Noah and her problems with her boss. She chose not to ignore him and sent a reply:

"Hey Ash."

His message came in relatively late:

"Nevermind."

Nothing else.

She sighed. Why was Ash doing this?

"Just say something, reply to my calls for goodness sake! Why're you acting up?" she yelled to the phone screen.

"Can I see you today Ash?
Please?"

Her pride had gone six feet into the ground when she'd typed this, so he'd better agree. In fact, he didn't have to agree, he'd better reply, for the sake of her self-respect. His chat showed typing, and she was relieved.

"Where?"

She pondered. Where?

"Your house?"

Seen.

"Fucking say something! Does that mean a yes?" She typed another message:

"That okay?"

Still, no reply. But luckily, he began typing again soon.

"Sure."

She got ready and headed to his house. When she got there, her fingers pushed the doorbell, and seconds later, the door opened, revealing a gorgeous looking army officer.

"Hello," she greeted awkwardly.

His eyes were low. "Why did you want to see me?"

She shrugged her shoulders. "Can't I just check up on you? We haven't talked in a while."

"Yeah, but I'm actually busy."

"Oh really? What, if I may ask, are you doing right now?" She crossed her arms.

"Is the questioning really necessary?" He scratched the back of his head. "Look, I'm sorry I haven't made out time to talk to you."

"You could have told me that!" she said. "I would totally understand. But then sometimes you were just being downright rude!"

"I'm sorry, Alecia."

Suddenly, all the urge she had to be mad at him vanished. Thanks to the velvety way her name rolled off his tongue. This was what he did to her. Using these uncanny charms to mess with her head, making her forget that she was meant to be angry. He could just tell her why he was behaving like this. She wanted to know if it was something she didn't know or if he just didn't like her like that. Her earlier conversation with her Dad came to mind suddenly. Should she ask him about his feelings for her directly?

But what if he rejects me?

"You said you didn't like people coming over, so why did you have a barbeque the other day?" she insisted.

"I didn't just have a barbeque. Lisa was celebrating her birthday, and she insisted on having it in my house. Something about the ambience."

"But why didn't you tell me?"

"I've noticed you don't like Lisa a lot."

Shit, it's that obvious?

His excuses were checking out, but she didn't know why she didn't feel convinced just yet. Ask him! the Alecia in her head pressurized, but she shut her out. She wasn't going to ask him any more questions.

"Okay, just please don't leave me hanging like that," she told him, and he smiled faintly. It didn't resemble his usual smiles, but hey, at least she got one.

When they were done talking, she turned back to leave, expecting him to suggest dropping her off, but he didn't do so. She kept walking forward, but he didn't stop her. Did he not want to spend more time with her? Oh goodness, what if he was pushing her away because of how clingy she was? But she couldn't control how she was. She trekked a distance before stopping and turning around, but Ash wasn't at the door anymore. He'd already gone inside. He hadn't even waited for her to leave. Now, she was convinced he didn't see her that way. What was she thinking? Why would she assume some guy she'd just met a month ago would be completely head over heels for her?

The only person capable of acting so stupidly and falling for someone so quickly was her. She shouldn't even be thinking of

him this way. She shouldn't. They may
have made love one night, but that didn't
mean they were in love. People did that all
the time. They'd go to a club, find a girl,
screw her for the night, and then, they'd go
their separate ways.

Her thoughts were only incurring her more
pain. Noah had tried to get away from her,
and so did Ash. Maybe she was the
problem. She'd never thought of that
before. But… she liked Ash so much. He'd
given her a new hope of being with
someone whose company she'd actually
loved; someone that made her feel like she

could be her real self around him. She couldn't just lose him like that.

But she also couldn't force herself on him.

Now, she was just jumping to conclusions. Ash might be acting strange now, but that didn't imply that he didn't like her. He was the same guy who'd always checked up on her and had come all the way from New Jersey just to spend the day with her. She couldn't keep assuming things, she had to find out for herself—from him. She turned around and walked back to his house. The stomping from her boots echoed through the deafening silence the night brought, and when she finally walked up his stairs again, her heart was pounding in her chest. She reached out to ring his doorbell.

Her mind played different scenarios of how Ash would possibly reject her, and she pulled her finger away. He could be indifferent to her emotions and tell her that he hadn't cared from the start—or he could act like Noah and make it look like it was all her fault. He might even find her feelings for him hilarious, telling her that there was no such relationship between them. Boys could be heartless. Her Dad had told her that as well.

But he'd also told her it was important she did this, so she braced herself, taking a deep breath and hovering her finger over the doorbell. Just push it, Alecia, she thought but pulled back and rethought what she was going to say. She looked back at the doorbell. Why was she fidgeting so much about this? She should just ask him to his face, hear whatever he had to say, and take it, good or bad. It was better to be heartbroken now. Her break was ending next week, and the thing she didn't want was Mr. Reynolds calling her 'unproductive' because of her moodiness at work.

She took a deep breath and pushed it, then winced like she'd just activated a time bomb. She heard his footsteps get close to the door, and her heart raced. Her hands turned cold when he unlocked it and opened it. He looked at her, and she watched as surprise crossed his handsome features. "You came back?"

"Yes, actually, I wanted to tell you something," she replied. "I mean, ask you something."

He looked at her seriously. "Go ahead."

The words were caught in her throat before she could manage to force them out. However, they came out as a stutter, "Ash, I-I want you to be honest with me."

Alecia couldn't remember the last time she'd been this nervous. Probably when she was meeting Ash for the first time, but that was nothing compared to what she was feeling now.

"Yeah, just ask," he said.

"I'm serious. Don't lie."

He nodded again. "Sure."

262

She took a deep breath. "Ash, you know about my ex-boyfriend and how he cheated on me. I would have been devastated if it weren't for you. So I'm really thankful for that."

He nodded. "You've told me about this before."

She continued, "Yes, but lately, you've been pushing me away, and it's really hurting me. If there's something wrong, you can tell me about it."

She paused. "Ash, I think I'm falling in love with you. I'm not lying! You're like the perfect guy. You make me feel safe and heard, and you let me be myself without trying to make me change. You even make me laugh more than anyone else has made me."

Okay, she was over-expressing now.

She avoided eye contact with him like it would kill her. "The point is, you're not really consistent with how you act. Sometimes you're perfect, and other times, you're so cold to me. Ash, I really like you, and I don't want to lose you, so I want to know if I'm just delusional for hoping anything can work out between us, because I really do."

She finally summoned the courage to look at him. He was staring at her with an emotion she couldn't quite make out. She wasn't sure if it was good or bad, but he appeared to be shocked by her confession.

She finally asked him, "Ash, I want to know what you want." She paused. "Do you like me that way as well?"

Made in the USA
Middletown, DE
23 July 2025

11100893R00150